GREAT ILLUSTRATED CLASSICS

ANNE OF GREEN GABLES

L. M. Montgomery

adapted by
Eliza Gatewood Warren

Illustrations by
Joseph Miralles

ABDO
Publishing Company

GREAT ILLUSTRATED CLASSICS

edited by
Joshua E. Hanft

visit us at
www.abdopub.com

Library edition published in 2002 by ABDO Publishing Company, 4940 Viking Drive, Suite 622, Edina, Minnesota 55435. Published by agreement with Playmore Incorporated Publishers and Waldman Publishing Corporation.

Library of Congress Cataloging-in-Publication Data

Montgomery, L.M. (Lucy Maud), 1874-1942.
 Anne of Green Gables / L.M.Montgomery; adapted by Eliza Gatewood Warren; illustrated by Joseph Miralles.
  p. cm – (Great illustrated classics)
 Reprint. Originally published: New York: Playmore: Waldman Pub., 1995.
 Summary: Anne, an eleven-year-old orphan, is sent by mistake to live with a lonely, middle-aged brother and sister on a Prince Edward Island farm and proceeds to make an indelible impression on everyone around her.
 ISBN 1-57765-816-7
 [1. Orphans--Fiction. 2. Friendship--Fiction. 3. Country life--Prince Edward Island--Fiction. 4. Prince Edward Island--Fiction.] I. Warren, Eliza Gatewood. II. Miralles, Joseph, ill. III. Title. IV. Series.

PZ7.M768 An 2002
[Fic]--dc21
                                                              2001055389

Contents

About The Author

Lucy Maud Montgomery was born on November 30, 1874 in Clifton (now New London) on Prince Edward Island, a province of Canada. Her mother died when she was a baby, and she was raised by her grandparents.

Young Lucy began writing short stories and verse as a child. Her first poem was published in the local paper when she was fifteen. In her late teens she qualified for a teacher's license at Prince of Wales College in Charlottetown and studied at Dalhousie University in Halifax, Nova Scotia. For three years she worked there as a journalist and teacher.

In 1898 the young career woman returned home to care for her grandmother who was ill. In her spare time she wrote short stories and poems for children's magazines.

Then one day Lucy was leafing through her notebook of plots for a short serial she had been asked to write for a Sunday School paper. A faded entry written years earlier caught her eye: "Elderly couple apply to orphanage for a boy. By mistake a girl is sent them." The result was her touching first novel, *Anne of Green Gables*. Six sequels which detail the marriage and career of the author's lovable heroine followed. They include *Anne of Avonlea*, *Chronicles of Avonlea*, *Anne's House of Dreams*, *Anne of the Island*, and *Anne of Windy Poplars*.

In 1911 the author married a minister, Reverend Ewan MacDonald, and moved to Toronto, Canada. However, she never stopped missing picturesque Prince Edward Island which is the scene of all but one of her twenty-one novels.

Anne of Green Gables, considered Lucy Montgomery's masterpiece, won her international acclaim. The book has been filmed, translated into five languages, and transcribed into Braille.

The recipient of numerous prestigious awards, the author died at 67 on April 24, 1942.

And Notice She Did!

Chapter One

The News is Shocking

Mrs. Rachel Lynde was a busybody who lived in Avonlea, a town on beautiful Prince Edward Island off Canada's Atlantic coast.

Now Avonlea occupied a little peninsula that jutted out, with water on both sides. It was impossible for any traveler on the hill road to pass in and out of town without Mrs. Rachel noticing. And notice she did! Every spare minute she had, she sat by her kitchen window knitting her "cotton warp" quilts and watching the comings and goings on the road.

One warm June afternoon, she was amazed

to see Matthew Cuthbert drive by. Not only was he using his buggy and sorrel mare, but he was wearing his best suit. All this led Mrs. Rachel to believe Matthew was traveling out of Avonlea—a fair distance, no doubt. Now where was Matthew Cuthbert going and why?

If it had been any other man in town, Mrs. Rachel would have known the answer to those questions. But Matthew was different from other folks. He was a shy man who never visited or ventured far from home. She felt certain that Matthew must be on an important mission.

"I'll just go over to Green Gables after tea and find out from Marilla what Matthew is up to," Mrs. Rachel muttered. "I want to get to the bottom of this mystery."

Green Gables, a large, rambling house set amid flowering orchards, was located a quarter mile up the road from Lynde's Hollow. When Mrs. Rachel arrived there later in the afternoon, Matthew's sister, Marilla, was sit-

He Was Wearing His Best Suit.

ting in her tidy kitchen knitting. Behind her, three plates were laid on the table.

Marilla must be expecting Matthew to bring someone home for tea, Mrs. Rachel thought. However, the dishes were everyday dishes and there were only crab apple preserves and one kind of cake. The company could not be anyone special. Yet what could explain Matthew's unusual appearance today?

"Good evening, Rachel," Marilla said. She was a tall, thin woman who wore her gray-streaked hair swept up in a bun on the back of her head. "Won't you sit down? How are all your folks?"

"We are all fine," Mrs. Rachel answered. "I was worried about you though, when I saw Matthew drive by earlier. I thought maybe he was going to get the doctor because you were ill."

"Oh, I'm quite well," Marilla told her, knowing full well how curious her nosy neighbor must be about Matthew's trip. "Matthew went

Expecting Someone for Tea

to Bright River. We are getting a little boy from an orphanage in Nova Scotia, and he's coming on the train tonight."

If Marilla had said that Matthew had gone to Bright River to meet a kangaroo from Australia, Mrs. Rachel could not have been more astonished. Nothing would ever surprise her again! Nothing! "What on earth put such a notion in your head, Marilla?" she demanded disapprovingly.

"We've been thinking of this all winter," Marilla said. "Mrs. Alexander Spencer was here before Christmas. She said she was going to get a little girl from the Hopeton orphanage in the spring. So Matthew and I decided to get a boy. We send word to Mrs. Spencer by her brother, Robert, to pick out someone about eleven who can help with the chores. Matthew is sixty years old now, and he's not as spry as he used to be. He has a slight heart condition, you know."

"Well, Marilla, I'll tell you right out I think

"He's Coming on the Train Tonight."

you're doing a risky thing. You're bringing a strange child into your house, and you don't know a thing about him. Why, only last week I read in the paper how a couple took in an orphan boy, and he set their house on fire. He nearly burned them to a crisp in their beds."

"I admit I've had some doubts myself, Rachel," Marilla told her neighbor, who was red in the face from her outburst. "But Matthew's mind was made up. I could see that, so I gave in."

"I hope it turns out all right," replied Mrs. Rachel anxiously. "Just the other day I heard about an orphan girl who put poison in her adopted family's well."

"We're not getting a girl," said Marilla, ignoring Mrs. Rachel's gloomy comment. "I'd never dream of raising a girl. So you see, Rachel, the matter is all settled."

Mrs. Rachel would have liked to stay at Green Gables until Matthew returned with his young charge, but that would have been a long

"I've Had Some Doubts Myself."

wait. She decided to drop by Robert Bell's house to tell this unbelievable news. It would certainly create sensations, and Mrs. Rachel loved to create a sensation. The truth was that Marilla was glad to see her leave.

"Well, of all things that ever were or will be," Mrs. Rachel said when she was safely out in the lane. "I'm sorry for that poor boy waiting at the station. Matthew and Marilla don't know anything about raising children. They will expect him to be wiser than his own grandfather. I just can't imagine a child at Green Gables! After all, there's never been one there before."

At the very moment she spoke those words, Matthew Cuthbert drove up to the Bright River station. At first he thought he was early. But the stationmaster told him the 5:30 train had come and gone. To his dismay, the young orphan boy he had come to meet was nowhere to be seen.

The only person in sight was a skinny, red-

"Imagine a Child at Green Gables!"

headed girl sitting straight and tall on a pile of shingles at the end of the station platform.

Matthew walked past her hurriedly, avoiding her gaze. Yet out of the corner of his eye, he could see that her hands were clasped tightly in front of her and that her body was tense and rigid. He had the feeling that this poor child was waiting anxiously for someone.

This Poor Child Was Waiting for Someone.

"A Passenger for You."

Chapter Two

A Difficult Homecoming

"There was a passenger dropped off for you," the stationmaster called out to Matthew. "That little girl sitting over there."

"I'm not expecting a girl," Matthew said nervously. Except for Marilla and Mrs. Rachel Lynde, women made him most uncomfortable. "I've come for a boy. Mrs. Alexander Spencer was to bring a boy over from Nova Scotia."

The stationmaster whistled. "Guess there's been some mistake. Mrs. Spencer got off with that girl and left her in my charge. Said you and your sister were adopting her and would be along for her soon."

For the first time, Matthew took a good look at the little waif who sat there on the shingles eyeing him. A freckle-faced child of about eleven, she was dressed in a short, drab yellow-grey dress and a faded brown sailor hat. Her bright red hair was plaited in two thick braids.

"I suppose you are Mr. Matthew Cuthbert of Green Gables," she piped up in a sweet voice. "I was beginning to fear you weren't coming for me. I had decided that if you didn't come tonight, I'd go down the track to that wild cherry tree and climb up in its white blossoms to sleep. I could imagine I was living in marble halls."

Matthew took her scrawny little hand in his. "I'm sorry I was late," he said shyly. He simply could not tell this child with the glowing eyes that there had been a mistake. Marilla would have to do that. "Come along," he said. "The horse is over in the yard. Give me your

Matthew Took a Good Look.

bag."

"Oh, I can carry it," the girl said cheerfully. "I'm so glad you've come. It seems so wonderful that I'm going to belong to you. I've never belonged to anybody before—not really."

Matthew and his charge reached the buggy and climbed in. As they left the village and made their way down a steep hill, they drove along a road fringed on either side with blooming wild cherry trees and white birches.

"Isn't this a beautiful sight?" his companion exclaimed. "What do these lacy white trees remind you of?"

"Well now, I dunno," Matthew replied.

"Why, a bride of course—all in white with a misty veil. I don't ever expect to be a bride because I'm too homely. But I have dreams of wearing pretty clothes someday. Why, only this morning I put on this ugly old dress and pretended it was a gorgeous blue silk gown. I was happy all the way over on the boat to Prince Edward Island. Oh, I never dreamed

Cherry Trees and White Birches

that I would get to live here. Tell me, why are all the roads red?"

"Well now, I dunno," Matthew answered.

"This is one of the things I shall have to find out," the newcomer said. "This is such an interesting world. It wouldn't be half as interesting if we knew all about everything, would it? Am I talking too much, Mr. Cuthbert? Mrs. Spencer says I do."

Much to his own surprise, Matthew was enjoying himself. Like most quiet folks, he liked talkative people, particularly this little girl who seemed to say the first thing that popped into her head. "Oh, you can talk as much as you like," he assured her. "I don't mind."

"Oh, I'm so glad," his new friend replied. "I know you and I are going to get along just fine."

As they drove the remainder of the eight miles to Green Gables, the young girl chatted on and on about the beautiful scenery.

At one point they drove through an archway

"Such an Interesting World."

of fragrant apple blossoms. Enchanted by the sight, the girl whispered, "Oh, Mr. Cuthbert, what was that place we just passed through?"

"We call it The Avenue," Matthew told her.

"Oh, it was wonderful," she cried. "It gave me a funny, sort of pleasant ache inside. Did you ever have an ache like that?"

"Well, now, I don't know that I have."

"The name Avenue just doesn't properly describe that stretch of road," she blurted out. "I'm going to rename it the White Way of Delight."

They drove over the crest of a hill and gazed at the pond below, its water a glory of many different colors. A bridge spanned it midway.

"That's Barry's Pond," Matthew said. "It's named for Mr. Barry who lives at Orchard Slope over there. He has a daughter, Diana—about your age, I think."

"Oh, I don't like the name Barry's Pond either. I shall change it to the Lake of Shining Waters because the water looks as if it's smil-

"The White Way of Delight"

ing up at me."

"We're almost home now," Matthew interrupted, looking down at her shining little face.

"That's Green Gables over there in the distance."

It was dark when Matthew pulled into the lane at Green Gables. With a heavy heart he escorted the eager girl into the house.

"Matthew Cuthbert," cried Marilla, running into the front hall to greet them. "Where is the boy?"

"There wasn't any boy," Matthew stammered, putting down the girl's suitcase. "There was only her."

"But there must have been a boy," Marilla insisted. "Mrs. Spencer was supposed to bring us a boy. This is a pretty piece of business."

Suddenly their visitor realized the truth of the situation. "You don't want me," she cried, dropping into a chair and sobbing uncontrollably. "Nobody ever did want me! I might have known the dream was too beautiful to last."

"Where is the Boy?"

"There's no need to cry," Marilla said.

"Yes, there is," the girl wailed. "You would cry, too, if you were an orphan and had come to a new home only to learn no one wanted you because you weren't a boy."

"Come now. Stop crying. You will spend the night with us, and then we'll investigate this matter tomorrow. What is your name?" Marilla asked.

"Will you please call me Cordelia?" the girl asked.

"Is that your name?" Marilla wanted to know.

"No," the girl admitted, "but I would like to be called Cordelia. It's such an elegant name."

"What is your real name?" Marilla asked.

"Anne Shirley," the girl replied. "Oh, why didn't you tell me at the station that you didn't want me, Mr. Cuthbert? If I hadn't seen the White Way of Delight and the Lake of Shining Waters, this wouldn't be so hard."

"What on earth does she mean?" Marilla

"You Would Cry Too."

asked, staring at Matthew.

"She's just referring to some conversation we had on our way here. Now, don't you think it's time we ate dinner?"

The three of them sat down at the dinner table, but Anne just picked at her food. "I can't eat," she told Matthew and Marilla. "I am in the depths of despair."

"I guess she's tired," Matthew said. "I think you better put her to bed, Marilla."

After Marilla tucked the tearful girl into bed in the east gable room, she had a long talk with Matthew in the kitchen.

"I will drive over to see Mrs. Alexander Spencer tomorrow," Marilla announced as she began washing the dishes. "That girl will have to be sent back to the orphanage."

"Yes, I suppose so," Matthew said quietly.

"You suppose so! Don't you know it?" Marilla fairly shouted.

"Well now, Marilla. She's a real nice little thing, and she does want to stay with us," he

But Anne Just Picked at Her Food.

said.

"What good would she be to us?" his sister asked.

"We might be some good to her," Matthew said unexpectedly.

"Matthew, this child has bewitched you. It's plain as plain you want to keep her," Marilla said.

"You should have heard her talk on the way over here," Matthew persisted. "She's a real interesting little thing."

"Look, Matthew," Marilla said. "I don't want an orphan girl, and if I did, I wouldn't want her. And that is my final word."

"What Good Would She Be?"

The Glorious World of Green Gables

Chapter Three

Marilla Is in a Dilemma

The next morning was a beautiful, warm June day drenched in sunshine. Anne simply refused to waste one minute being unhappy.

She jumped out of bed and threw open the windows and gazed in awe at the glorious world of Green Gables. An apple orchard bloomed on one side of the house and a cherry grove on the other. In the distance, fields of grass were sprinkled with dandelions and clover. Gardens blossomed with fragrant lilacs, and a brook meandered lazily through the property. Off to the left, Anne spotted two big barns, and on the horizon she glimpsed the sparkling blue sea.

"What a lovely place," she murmured. "I could imagine living here forever."

At breakfast she told Marilla she didn't dare go outside. "If I go outside and explore Green Gables, I won't be able to stop loving it. It's hard enough now, and I don't want to make it any harder. I know you don't want to keep me because I'm not a boy."

"I never in all my life saw or heard anything to equal her," muttered Marilla, beating a retreat down the cellar stairs after potatoes. "She will say just anything! First thing you know, she'll be casting a spell over me, too."

Late in the afternoon a determined Marilla took Anne in the buggy to visit Mrs. Alexander Spencer in White Sands and straighten out the misunderstanding that had occurred.

"I'm sure Mrs. Spencer will make arrangements to send Anne back to the orphanage," she said to Matthew as she drove off. It was

On the Way to White Sands

hard to ignore the wistful expression on his face.

"I've made up my mind to enjoy the trip," Anne said as they rode along. "I'm not going to think about returning to the orphanage. I'm just going to think about the drive. Are we going across the Lake of Shining Waters today?"

"We're not going over Barry's Pond if that's what you mean by your Lake of Shining Waters," Marilla said. "We're going along the shore road. Since it's five miles to White Sands, why don't you use this time to tell me about yourself—not your imaginings—but the facts."

"I am eleven years old," Anne began. "I was born in Bolingbroke, Nova Scotia to Walter and Bertha Shirley. My father was a high school teacher, but they were very poor and died of the fever when I was only four months old. Since there were no relatives nearby, a Mrs. Thomas took me. But she was poor, too,

"I Am Eleven Years Old," Anne Began.

and had a drunken husband. I lived with them until I was eight. When Mr. Thomas died, his mother gave Mrs. Thomas and the kids a home. But she didn't want me."

"I see," said Marilla quietly. "Who did you live with after that?"

"A Mrs. Hammond from up the river," Anne explained. "She needed someone to help with her twins. She had three sets, you see. When her husband died, the family was split up. I was sent to that awful orphanage where I lived for four months until Mrs. Spencer came and picked me."

"Were those women—Mrs. Thomas and Mrs. Hammond—good to you?" asked Marilla, looking at Anne out of the corner of her eye.

"Oh," faltered Anne sadly. "They meant to be. They had a lot to worry them, you know. It's very hard to have a drunken husband and twins three times. But I'm sure they meant to be."

What a sad, unhappy life this child has had,

"Were Those Women Good to You?"

Marilla thought. No wonder she was so delighted at the prospect of a real home. Maybe I *should* indulge Matthew's whim and let her stay. I must say she's very ladylike and nice. She talks too much, but she could be trained out of that.

When they arrived at Mrs. Spencer's big yellow house in White Sands, she seemed surprised to see them. "Dear, dear," she exclaimed. "You're the last folks I was looking for today. But I'm real glad to see you."

"I'm afraid a mistake has been made, and I've come to get to the bottom of it," Marilla stated. "Matthew and I sent you word by your brother to bring us a boy from the orphanage."

"Marilla Cuthbert, you don't say," cried Mrs. Spencer in distress. "Why, Robert sent word down by his daughter, Nancy, and she said that you wanted a girl, didn't he, Flora Jean?" She turned and looked intently at her daughter who had come to the steps.

"She certainly did, Miss Cuthbert," Flora

Mrs. Spencer's Big Yellow House

Jean answered earnestly.

"I'm dreadfully sorry," said Mrs. Spencer. "It's too bad, but it wasn't my fault. I thought I was following your instructions."

"It was our own fault," Marilla said. "We should not have allowed an important message to be passed along by word of mouth. Can we send this child back to the orphanage?"

"Yes, you can, but I don't think that will be necessary," Mrs. Spencer informed her. "Mrs. Peter Blewett was here yesterday wishing for a little girl to help her with her large family. Anne would be the perfect child for her."

Marilla knew she should be grateful for the opportunity to get this unwelcome orphan off her hands, but for some reason this news was very unsettling. Mrs. Blewett had a reputation for having a bad temper and a stingy nature. Her children were supposed to be very naughty, too.

"This is your lucky day," exclaimed Mrs. Spencer. "Here is Mrs. Blewett coming up the

"Can We Send This Child Back?"

lane now. Why don't all of you move into the parlor and have a seat? You take the armchair, Miss Cuthbert, and you sit on the ottoman, Anne, but don't wiggle. Flora Jean, you go put the buns in the oven."

Mrs. Blewett stormed into the room and plopped down on the sofa.

"Good afternoon, Mrs. Blewett," Mrs. Spencer said. "We just were saying how fortunate it was you happened along. Let me introduce you to Miss Cuthbert and Anne Shirley."

Anne sat mutely on the ottoman with her hands clasped tightly in her lap, staring at Mrs. Blewett. Was she really going to have to live with this sharp-faced, sharp-eyed woman? She felt a lump in her throat and tears stinging her eyes.

"It seems there's been a mistake about this little girl, Mrs. Blewett," Mrs. Spencer explained. "I was under the impression that Mr. and Miss Cuthbert wanted to adopt a girl. I was certainly told so. But it seems it was a boy

Mrs. Blewett Stormed Into the Room.

they wanted. So if you still would like to have a girl, Anne would be just the one for you."

"Humph. You don't look like there's much to you," Mrs. Blewett barked at Anne. "If I take you, you will have to earn your keep. I need a lot of help with the new baby. He cries all the time. I'm just clean worn out taking care of him."

Marilla looked at Anne's pale face and rose to her feet. "Just a minute, Mrs. Blewett. Before you say another word, I have an announcement to make."

Marilla Rose to Her Feet.

"It'll Have to," Mrs. Blewett Snapped.

Chapter Four

Anne Learns Marilla's Decision

"I have decided to take Anne home overnight and talk this situation over with Matthew again," Marilla said slowly. "After all, I never said we wouldn't keep Anne. I just came here to find out how the mistake was made. If we make up our minds not to keep her, we'll bring her over to you tomorrow night, Mrs. Blewett. If we don't, you know Anne is going to stay with us. Will that suit you?"

"I suppose it'll have to," Mrs. Blewett snapped.

During Marilla's speech, Anne's eyes grew

deep and bright as morning stars. When Mrs. Spencer and Mrs. Blewett went out to the kitchen, she flew to Marilla's side. "Oh, Miss Cuthbert, did you really say that perhaps you would let me stay at Green Gables?" she whispered. "Or did I only imagine that you did?"

"I think you better learn to control your imagination, Anne, so you know what's real and what isn't," Marilla answered crossly. "Yes, you did hear me say that and no more. It isn't decided yet, and perhaps we will let Mrs. Blewett take you. After all, she certainly needs you more than I do."

"I'd rather go back to the orphanage than go live with her," Anne cried. "She looks like . . . like . . . a real shrew!"

"You should be ashamed of yourself for talking badly about a lady like Mrs. Blewett," Marilla replied, smothering a smile. "Come along, Anne. We must go home."

When they arrived back at Green Gables that evening, Matthew met them in the lane.

"Perhaps You'll Let Me Stay?"

He seemed relieved to see that Anne had returned.

Later when they were behind the barn milking cows, Marilla told him about Anne's tragic past and the results of her interview with Mrs. Spencer.

"I wouldn't give a dog to that Blewett woman," Matthew said vehemently.

"Well, I certainly agree with you, Matthew. But it's either Mrs. Blewett or us. Since you seem so set on taking Anne, I guess I'm willing. I've never brought up a child, especially a girl, but I'll do my best."

Matthew's face glowed with delight. "Well, Marilla, I reckoned you'd come to see it that way. She's such an interesting little thing."

"I'd be much happier if you could say she was a useful thing," retorted Marilla. "But I'll make it my business to train her to be. And mind you, Matthew, you're not to interfere with my methods. Maybe an old maid doesn't know much about raising a child, but she

Behind the Barn

knows more than an old bachelor. So you just let me manage her."

"Have it your way, Marilla," Matthew said. "Only be as good and kind to her as you can without spoiling her. I really think you could do anything with her if you got her to love you."

Marilla didn't tell Anne that they had decided to keep her until the next afternoon. All that morning she kept her busy doing various chores and observed her progress. By noon she had concluded that Anne was bright and obedient, willing to work and quick to learn. Her only fault seemed to be her tendency to daydream on the job.

When Anne had finished the lunch dishes, she suddenly confronted Marilla. "Oh, Miss Cuthbert, I've been patient all morning, but I really must know if you're going to send me away."

"Well," said Marilla, "I suppose I might as well tell you that Matthew and I have decided

Her Tendency to Daydream

to keep you, that is, if you will try to be a good girl. Why, child, whatever is the matter?"

"I'm crying," said a bewildered Anne. "I can't think why. I'm glad as glad can be. But glad isn't quite the right word. I was glad about the White Way and the cherry blossoms. But now I'm more than glad. I'm so happy. It will be up-hill work to be good. Mrs. Thomas often told me I was desperately wicked. But can you tell me why I'm crying?"

"I suppose it's because you're so excited," Marilla said. "Now sit down and try to relax. We are going to try and raise you right. First of all, I want you to go to Sunday School and learn your prayers. You can start this afternoon by memorizing the Lord's Prayer. And secondly, you will go to elementary school in the fall. And one more thing, I want you to call me Marilla and not Miss Cuthbert."

"Oh, this is all so wonderful," Anne cried. "I could pretend I was Lady Cordelia all dressed up in a gown of white lace with a pearl cross

"Glad as Glad Can Be"

on my chest and pearls in my hair. But no, I am Anne of Green Gables, and that is so much better than being Anne of anywhere. Oh, and I do so want to have a best friend here in Avonlea. Do you think that is possible, Marilla?"

"Maybe so," Marilla answered thoughtfully. "Diana Barry lives over at Orchard Slope and she's about your age. Right now she's away visiting her aunt in Carmody. But hopefully you will get acquainted when she returns. In the meantime, you'll be meeting some of my friends."

Mrs. Rachel Lynde was the first person in Avonlea to come to Green Gables to meet Anne. When Mrs. Rachel arrived, Anne was outside on one of her many exploring trips around the farm.

"It was too bad a mistake was made about the adoption," Mrs. Rachel told Marilla. "Couldn't you have sent the girl back?"

"Yes," Marilla replied. "But Matthew had taken a fancy to her, and I grew to like her, too.

"I Am Anne of Green Gables."

This house is a different place now that she's here. Oh, look, Rachel, here comes Anne now."

"Well, they didn't pick you for your looks," Mrs. Rachel said when Anne came flying in the door. "What a skinny, homely girl you are! Did you ever see such freckles and bright red hair?"

"You are a rude, nasty woman and fat, too!" Anne screamed, stamping her foot on the floor. "I hate you, Mrs. Rachel. I hate you!" She burst into tears and fled from the room.

"They Didn't Pick You for Your Looks."

"I Don't Envy You."

Chapter Five

The Apology

"Well, I don't envy you your job of bringing up that girl, Marilla," said Mrs. Rachel, glaring indignantly at her friend.

"You shouldn't have ridiculed her about her looks, Rachel," Marilla answered, amazed at her own response.

"Marilla Cuthbert, you aren't defending her after that terrible display of temper, are you?"

"No," said Marilla slowly. "She's been naughty, and I will have to talk to her about it. But she's never been taught what's right. And you were too hard on her, Rachel."

"Well, I can see that I'll have to be very careful what I say after this since the feelings of orphans have to be considered before anything else. I'll be on my way now. Don't expect me to come hurrying back here though."

When Mrs. Rachel finally left, Marilla rushed up to the east gable room where she found Anne facedown on the bed crying bitterly.

"Anne," she said, "get off that bed this minute. That was a nice way for you to behave! Why did you have to insult Mrs. Rachel Lynde of all people?"

"She hadn't any right to call me ugly and red-headed," wailed Anne.

"You didn't have any right to fly into such a rage and talk the way you did to her. I was ashamed of you," said Marilla.

"Just imagine how you'd feel if somebody told you that you were skinny and ugly," pleaded Anne tearfully.

"It's true Rachel is much too frank," Marilla

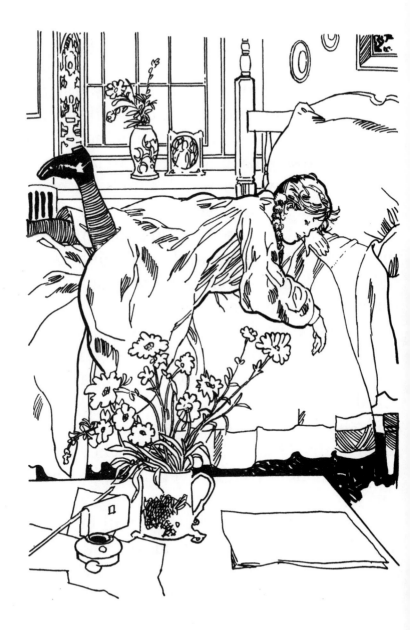

Anne Was Crying Bitterly.

said in a softer tone. "But she was a stranger, an older person, and my visitor—all three good reasons for you to be respectful of her. You simply must apologize and ask her to forgive you."

"I could never do that," said a determined Anne. "You can punish me any way you like. You can shut me up in a dark, damp dungeon inhabited by snakes and toads and feed me only bread and water, but I will not ask Mrs. Rachel to forgive me."

"I guess I won't put you in a dungeon," said Marilla. "But apologize you must. You'll stay here in your room until you change your mind."

"I shall stay here forever then," said Anne mournfully. "I can't tell Mrs. Rachel I'm sorry when I'm not. I can't even imagine that I'm sorry."

"Perhaps your imagination will be working better in the morning," said Marilla, rising to leave. "You will have the night to think over your conduct and change your mind."

"Punish Me Any Way You Like."

When Anne stayed stubbornly in her room during breakfast, Marilla had to tell Matthew the whole story.

"It's a good thing Rachel Lynde got a talking to. She's a meddlesome old gossip," Matthew said.

"Matthew, I'm surprised at you. You know Anne's behavior was dreadful, and yet you take her part. Do you think she shouldn't be punished at all?" Marilla asked.

"I reckon she ought to be punished a little," Matthew conceded. "But don't be too hard on her."

Despite the fact Marilla carried Anne's meals to her room on a tray, the girl ate very little, and she didn't leave the room.

That evening when Marilla went out to bring the cows back from the pasture, Matthew slipped in the house and crept upstairs. He tiptoed down the hall and stood for a few minutes outside the east gable room. Then he opened the door and peeked in.

Marilla Had to Tell Matthew.

Anne was sitting by the window looking very small and unhappy. Softly Matthew closed the door and went over to her. "How are you doing, Anne?" he whispered.

"Pretty well. I imagine a great deal, and that helps pass the time," she said.

"Don't you think you'd better apologize to Mrs. Rachel Lynde and get it over with? You know how determined Marilla is about this."

"I admit that I have calmed down overnight, and I am sorry now," Anne said sweetly. "I suppose I could apologize for you. Do you really want me to?"

"Of course I do. It's terribly lonesome downstairs without you. Just go and smooth it over—that's a good girl. But don't tell Marilla I said a word. She might think I was interfering, and I promised I wouldn't." With that, Matthew fled hastily outdoors to the remotest corner of the cow pasture.

When Marilla returned to the house, Anne announced that she was ready to make the

Matthew Went Over to Her.

apology.

Mrs. Rachel was knitting by her kitchen window when her visitors arrived on their important mission. "Come on in," she called.

Once inside, Anne fell to her knees and cried, "Oh, Mrs. Rachel, I'm extremely sorry. I behaved terribly to you, and I've disgraced my dear friends, Matthew and Marilla. It was very wicked of me to fly into a temper because you told me the truth. My hair is red, and I'm freckled and skinny and ugly. Oh, Mrs. Rachel, please forgive me."

Mrs. Rachel didn't notice that Anne was putting on a performance and enjoying every minute of it. "There, there, child. Of course I forgive you. I guess I am a terribly outspoken person. You mustn't mind me. You know I went to school with a girl with bright red hair like yours. When she grew up, her hair turned a handsome auburn color. I wouldn't be surprised if yours did, too—not a bit."

"Oh, Mrs. Rachel," Anne said in a long

Their Important Mission

breath as she rose to her feet. "You have given me real hope. I shall always consider you my benefactor and friend. I could endure anything if only I thought my hair would be a handsome auburn when I grow up."

"I apologized pretty well, didn't I?" Anne asked Marilla on the way home. She bent over to smell the white narcissi Mrs. Rachel had given her when they said good-bye.

"You did it quite thoroughly," Marilla agreed, secretly amused. "I hope you will try to control your temper in the future."

"That wouldn't be hard if people wouldn't tease me about my looks and make me mad," Anne remarked with a sigh.

"You shouldn't worry so much about your looks. Pretty is as pretty does," Marilla reminded her.

Far up in the shadows a light gleamed out through the trees from the kitchen at Green Gables. Suddenly, Anne slipped her hand into Marilla's. "It's lovely to be going home and

On the Way Home

know it's home," she said. "Marilla, I'm so happy."

Something warm and pleasant welled up in Marilla's heart at the touch of Anne's hand—a feeling of motherhood she had missed until now.

"Hurry along, Anne," the older woman urged. "I have a surprise waiting for you at Green Gables."

A Surprise Waiting at Green Gables

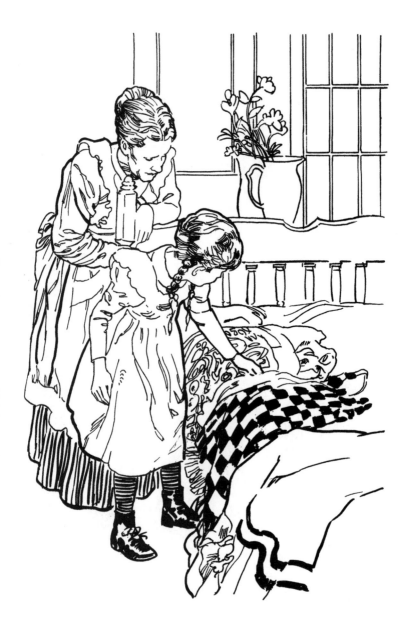

"How Do You Like Them?"

Chapter Six

The Joy of a New Friendship

"How do you like them?" asked Marilla.

Anne was standing in the gable room looking down at three new dresses spread out on the bed. One was a dreary brown gingham. Another was a black-and-white checked sateen, and the third was a stiff print in an ugly blue shade. Marilla had made the dresses herself, and they were all extremely plain.

"I'll try to imagine that I like them," said Anne slowly.

"You don't like them. I can tell," Marilla replied, offended. "What's wrong with them?"

"They're—they're not—pretty," said Anne slowly, trying not to hurt Marilla's feelings.

"Pretty!" Marilla cried. "I didn't go to all that trouble just to make pretty dresses for you. Those are good, sensible gowns that I expect you to take good care of. I should think you'd be grateful after all those skimpy things you've been wearing."

"But I am grateful," insisted Anne. "But I'd be ever so much gratefuller if—if you'd make just one with puffed sleeves. They're so fashionable."

"I think puffed sleeves are ridiculous looking," Marilla replied, looking down at her own simple dress. "I prefer plain, sensible sleeves."

"But I'd rather look ridiculous with everybody else than plain and sensible all by myself," persisted Anne sadly.

"I expect you to hang up those dresses carefully and then sit down and learn your Sunday lesson. Tomorrow will be your first day," was Marilla's only reply as she marched out the

"They're—They're Not—Pretty."

door.

The next morning Marilla had a bad headache, so Anne set off on her own for church, wearing the stiff black-and-white sateen dress and a plain, flat sailor hat. At the main road, she picked some buttercups and wild pink roses and adorned her hat with a heavy wreath of them.

Unfortunately, Anne had a miserable time at Sunday School and church. All the girls, who were dressed in pastel-colored dresses with puffed sleeves, stared at her flower-laden hat and began whispering and giggling behind her back. Not one person came up to her to say hello.

To make matters worse, Miss Rogerson, her Sunday School teacher, Mr. Bell who gave the opening prayer, and Mr. Bentley who delivered the sermon, were all long-winded and dull. When Anne came home very dejected, Marilla had to admit that some of her complaints were true.

She Picked Buttercups and Roses.

Gossip about Anne and her funny hat filtered back to Marilla by the next Friday. Mrs. Rachel Lynde wasted no time in making sure she knew that Anne had not made a good impression at church. Although Marilla was embarrassed, she took steps to get Anne's mind off the unpleasant incident.

"Cheer up, Anne," Marilla said. "I've got some good news for you. Diana Barry came home today. I'm going to see if I can borrow a skirt pattern from Mrs. Barry. Why don't you come along and meet Diana?"

"Oh, Marilla, I'm scared. What if she doesn't like me?" Anne asked, suddenly tensing inside.

"I'm sure Diana will like you just fine," Marilla assured her. "It's her mother you have to reckon with. If she has heard about your outburst with Mrs. Rachel and the buttercup bedecked hat you wore to church, I don't know what she'll think of you. You better be very polite and well-behaved. Let's be on our way

"What If She Doesn't Like Me?"

now."

They went over to Orchard Slope, taking a short cut across a brook and up the fir-covered hill grove.

Mrs. Barry came to the kitchen door and invited them in. "This is my daughter, Diana," she said, ushering her guests into the living room.

Diana, a pretty little girl with her mother's black eyes and hair, was sitting on the sofa reading a book. "Hello," she said, smiling.

"Diana, you might take Anne out in the garden and show her your flowers. Diana reads entirely too much," Mrs. Barry added to Marilla as the girls left the room.

Outside in the garden Anne and Diana stared at each other over a clump of orange tiger lilies.

"Oh, Diana," said Anne suddenly, clasping her hands and speaking almost in a whisper, "do you think you could like me a little—enough to be my best friend?"

Diana Was on the Sofa Reading.

"Why, I guess I could," Diana said. "I'm really awfully glad you've come to Green Gables. It will be wonderful to have someone to play with."

"Do you swear to be my best friend forever?" demanded Anne.

"It's dreadfully wicked to swear, you know," said Diana.

"You don't have to say any bad words," Anne softened her request. "All you have to do is take a solemn vow."

"I don't mind doing that," Diana replied, much relieved. "How do we do it?"

"We must join hands," Anne said gravely. "And we should do it over water. We'll just pretend that this path is running water. I'll take my oath first. I do solemnly swear to be faithful to my best friend, Diana Barry, as long as the sun and moon shall endure. Now you take your vow and use my name."

Diana repeated the oath, and the two new friends parted with many promises to spend

"Do You Swear?"

the next afternoon together.

"I'm the happiest girl on Prince Edward Island," Anne confided to Marilla on the way home. "Diana and I are going to build a playhouse in Mr. William Bell's birch grove tomorrow. Can I have those broken pieces of china that are out in the woodshed? Diana is going to show me a place back in the woods where rice lilies grow, and she is going to teach me to sing a song called 'Nelly in the Hazel Dell'," she added after taking a deep breath.

"I do hope that you won't talk Diana to death," said Marilla. "Please remember when you make your plans that you have your work to do. It'll have to be done before you play with Diana."

The days that followed were a happy time for Anne. She spent endless hours playing make-believe games with Diana in their woodland house they named Idlewild. As the friendship between the two girls flourished, Matthew and Marilla were delighted to see

The Happiest Girl on Prince Edward Island

how generous and kind their Anne was to her friend.

One night as Marilla sat darning socks in the sitting room with Matthew, she expressed a deep concern she had about her new daughter. "Anne's really a wonderful girl, but she is different. I do hope she's going to fit in with the other children at school when it opens in September," she said. "I do so want her to be happy."

She Expressed a Deep Concern.

"I'm Dreadfully Behind."

Chapter Seven

A Stormy Encounter at School

Despite Marilla's misgivings, Anne got off to a good start. "I think I'm going to really like school here in Avonlea," she told Marilla after the first day. "I get to sit with Diana right by the window, so we can look out and see the Lake of Shining Water. There are a lot of nice girls at school, but of course I like Diana best."

"How did you like your courses?" Marilla asked.

"I'm dreadfully behind, I'm afraid," Anne said frankly. "I'll have to work hard to catch up. Mr. Phillips, our teacher—I don't like him too much—already started us on reading, spelling, geography, and Canadian history. That I did like."

So it was that the first three weeks of school sailed quickly by. At the end of September, Gilbert Blythe, who had been visiting his cousins in New Brunswick all summer, returned to Avonlea and joined his class.

Diana explained to Anne that Gilbert, a handsome young boy with curly brown hair, hazel eyes, and a dazzling smile, had a reputation for being a terrible tease. As luck would have it, he sat right across the aisle from Anne.

The first day Gilbert was back, Anne glanced over and was shocked to see him pin the long yellow braid of Ruby Gillis, who sat in front of him, to the back of her seat. When Ruby got up, she fell back into her chair with a shriek, thinking her hair had been pulled out at the roots. Mr. Phillips glared at her so sternly that poor Ruby began to cry. Gilbert looked

Anne Was Shocked.

over at Anne and winked.

"I think your Gilbert Blythe is very hand-some," Anne confided to Diana later, "but he has a lot of nerve. Imagine him winking at me—a complete stranger."

That afternoon Mr. Philips was in a corner explaining an algebra problem to Prissy An-drews, while the rest of the class were doing pretty much as they pleased. Gilbert Blythe tried repeatedly to get Anne's attention, but she was lost in an exciting daydream.

Now Gilbert was not used to a girl ignoring him. He reached across the aisle, picked up the end of Anne's long red braid, held it at arm's length, and whispered loudly, "Carrots! Car-rots!"

Enraged, Anne sprang to her feet and ex-claimed, "Gilbert, you mean, hateful boy! How dare you talk to me like that!" And then— thwack! She picked up her slate and cracked it over the astonished boy's head.

"Oh," everyone said in horrified delight.

And Then—Thwack!

Diana gasped. Ruby Gillis, who was inclined to be hysterical anyway, began to cry.

A red-faced Mr. Phillips stalked quickly down the aisle. "Anne Shirley, what is the meaning of this outburst?" he demanded.

"It was my fault, Mr. Phillips. I teased her," Gilbert said before Anne could utter a word.

But Mr. Phillips completely ignored Gilbert's remark. "I'm sorry to see a student of mine display such a temper and mean spirit," he said in a solemn tone. "Anne, go stand on the platform in front of the blackboard for the rest of the afternoon."

Above her head he wrote, "Anne Shirley has a very bad temper. Anne Shirley must learn to control her temper."

Anne stood on the platform till school was over, still furious with Gilbert Blythe. Not only did she refuse to accept the apology he made on the way out, but she told Diana she would never forgive him.

"You mustn't mind Gilbert for making fun of

Mr. Phillips Stalked Quickly Down the Aisle.

your hair," Diana said soothingly. "Why, he pokes fun at all the girls. He laughs at my hair because it's so black and calls me a crow all the time."

"There's a big difference between being called a crow and being called carrots," Anne insisted. "Gilbert Blythe has hurt my feelings excruciatingly, Diana."

The entire matter might have blown over if nothing else had happened. However, the next day at lunch time the students were picking gum in Mr. Bell's spruce grove as they often did. Usually they were careful to keep an eye open for Mr. Phillips who lived nearby, so they could hurry back to school before he did.

Unfortunately, this particular day the boys and girls lingered too long in the grove and made it back to school just seconds after the the teacher. Anne, her hair wreathed with lilies, had been dancing alone in the woods like a sprite. Arms flying, she dashed into class the last one.

Mr. Bell's Spruce Grove

Since Mr. Phillips didn't want to punish a dozen tardy students, he chose Anne. "Take those silly flowers out of your hair and go sit with Gilbert Blythe," he ordered. "Did you hear me?"

Anne rose haughtily, stepped across the aisle, and sat down beside Gilbert Blythe. Then she buried her face in her arms on the desk for the rest of the afternoon. To Anne, this was the end. It was bad enough to be singled out for punishment from among a dozen equally guilty classmates, but worse to be forced to sit with Gilbert. Never had she felt such shame.

When school was over, Anne removed everything from her desk—books, writing tablet, pen and ink—and stacked them on her cracked slate.

"Why are you taking these things home, Anne?" asked Diana as soon as they were out on the road.

"I'm not going back to school, that's why!"

She Buried Her Face in Her Arms.

ANNE OF GREEN GABLES

Anne exclaimed.

Diana gasped. "Will Marilla let you stay home?"

"She'll have to," Anne said. "I'll never go back to school or to that man again!"

"I'll Never Go Back to School!"

"Humor Anne a Little."

Chapter Eight

Anne's Tea Party Is a Disaster

When Anne announced her decision not to go back to school, Marilla tried everything in her power to persuade her differently. She even consulted her friend, Mrs. Rachel Lynde, who had raised ten children.

Mrs. Rachel had heard the whole story from Tillie Boulter. Apparently all the students rather liked Anne and had taken her side.

"My advice to you," said Mrs. Rachel, who loved to give advice, "is to humor Anne a little. After all, it sounds like Mr. Phillips was in the wrong."

"Then you really think I'd better let her stay home?" asked Marilla in amazement.

"Yes," Mrs. Rachel replied. "I wouldn't mention school to Anne again until she brings it up. Depend upon it, Marilla, she'll cool off in about a week and will go back to school on her own. If you were to force her, dear knows what tantrum she'd throw, and you'd have more trouble than ever."

Marilla decided to follow Mrs. Rachel's advice and busy herself with her own affairs. "I'm going to a meeting of the Ladies' Aid Society in Carmody this afternoon," she told Anne one morning. "Why don't you invite Diana over for tea?"

"Oh, Marilla," Anne exclaimed. "How perfectly lovely. I see you are learning to imagine things, too, or else you'd never have understood how I've longed for this very thing. Can I use the rosebud spray tea set?"

"The rosebud spray tea set! Well, what next? You know I never use that except on special oc-

"How Perfectly Lovely."

casions. You'll use the old brown tea set. But you can open up that crock of cherry preserves and cut some fruitcake, too."

"Can we sit in the parlor?" Anne asked.

"No, the sitting room will do for you and your company. You might like that raspberry cordial from the last church social. It's on the second shelf of the closet." And Marilla left.

The afternoon tea was held began in a very grand, formal manner. Diana arrived at the front door right on time, and Anne ushered her into the sitting room where they chatted like ladies.

Diana told Anne how much everyone at school missed her and wished she'd come back. Then she related all the news about their classmates. However, when she mentioned Gilbert Blythe's name, Anne jumped up and suggested they have some raspberry cordial.

Anne looked on the second shelf of the closet but didn't see the bottle there. Finally she spied it on the top shelf, put it on a tray, and

Anne Suggested Some Cordial.

set it on the table with a tumbler. "Now, please help yourself, Diana," she urged. "I'll wait awhile because I had some apple juice before you came."

"My, this raspberry cordial is delicious," Diana exclaimed, drinking one glass and pouring herself a second. "Marilla certainly is a good cook."

"Yes, she is," Anne agreed. "Now she's trying to teach me to be a good cook and hostess, but I'm afraid I'm a great trial to her. Last Tuesday we had some plum pudding and sauce left over after dinner. Marilla asked me to set it in the pantry and cover it. Only I forgot until the next morning. You can imagine my horror in finding that a mouse had drowned in the pudding sauce."

"Oh my," cried Diana, pouring herself a third glass of raspberry cordial. "What did you do?"

"I lifted the mouse out of the sauce with a spoon and threw it out in the yard. I meant to

"My, This is Delicious."

tell Marilla about it, but I forgot. Then that night she had Mr. and Mrs. Charles Ross to dinner. Everything went smoothly until dessert when Marilla walked into the dining room with the plum pudding and warmed up sauce. I stood up and shrieked, 'Marilla, you mustn't serve that pudding sauce. I forgot to tell you a mouse drowned in it.' Marilla turned red as fire, carried the pudding and sauce out, and brought in some strawberries. Later she gave me a terrible scolding. Why, Diana, what is the matter?" she added, staring at her friend.

Diana stood up unsteadily. Then she sat down again, putting her hands to her head. "I'm awfully sick," she said thickly. "I must go home."

"But you haven't had your tea," Anne said, "or the fruitcake or cherry preserves."

"I must go home," Diana repeated. "I'm terribly dizzy."

With a heavy heart, Anne walked with

"I Must Go Home."

Diana as far as the Barrys' yard fence where they said good-bye. Anne's elegant tea party was over. On Monday Marilla sent Anne to Mrs. Rachel's on an errand. It wasn't long before Anne, tears streaming down her face, came flying home. "Mrs. Rachel was at Orchard Slope today and said Mrs. Barry was fit to be tied. She says I got Diana drunk and that she's never going to let her play with me again. All I gave her was the raspberry cordial."

"Drunk fiddlesticks!" said Marilla, marching to the sitting room closet. There on the shelf sat a bottle of her homemade currant wine. Suddenly she remembered that she had stored the raspberry cordial in the basement, not the sitting room, as she had told Anne.

Marilla went back to the kitchen with the wine bottle in her hand. "Anne, you have a genius for getting into trouble. You gave Diana the currant wine instead of the cordial. Didn't you know the difference?"

"I never tasted it," said Anne. "I thought I

"Fiddlesticks!"

was serving the cordial. I was just trying to be hospitable. I would never deliberately get my best friend drunk."

Despite the fact that both Marilla and Anne visited Orchard Slope and tried to impress upon Mrs. Barry that Anne had made an innocent mistake, the obstinate woman refused to listen. She remained absolutely firm in her decision that Diana could never play with Anne again.

The following Monday Anne surprised Marilla by returning to school. "School is all that's left for me in life now that Diana and I have parted company," she explained.

Anne was welcomed back to school with open arms. She flung herself into her studies and made rapid progress. A tremendous rivalry developed between Anne and Gilbert Blythe, who was as good-natured about it as Anne was intense. By the end of the term they were both promoted to the fifth grade.

One by one the months slipped slowly by.

With Open Arms

One cold January night when Marilla and Mrs. Rachel had gone to Charlottetown to hear a speech by the Canadian premier, Anne and Matthew were reading together at the kitchen table.

Suddenly they heard the sound of flying footsteps on the icy walk outside, and the next moment the kitchen door flew open. In rushed Diana Barry white-faced and breathless.

"Oh Anne," she cried. "My sister is desperately ill with croup, and Mother and Father are away. Do come quick. I'm scared to death!"

"I'm Scared to Death!"

"The Doctors Are Both Away."

Chapter Nine

A Happy Reunion

Without a word Matthew reached for his cap and coat, slipped past Diana, and rushed outside into the dark night.

"He's gone to harness the sorrel mare to go to Carmody for the doctor," said Anne, quickly putting on her jacket. "Matthew and I are such kindred spirits that I can read his thoughts."

"I don't believe he'll find any doctors in Carmody," sobbed Diana. "I think they're both away in Charlottetown. And Mary Joe, our nanny, doesn't know anything about croup."

"Don't cry, Di," said Anne to cheer her up. "I know exactly what to do for croup. Don't forget that Mrs. Hammond had twins three times, and they all had croup regularly. Just wait till I get that ipecac bottle. Come on now."

When they reached Orchard Slope, Anne took one look at Diana's three year old sister, Minny May, and saw she was terribly sick. Feverish and restless, she lay on the kitchen sofa breathing hoarsely. Young Mary Joe, a broad-faced French girl Mrs. Barry had hired to care for the children, was completely bewildered.

Without wasting a minute, Anne went right to work. "Minny May has croup all right," she declared. "She's pretty sick, but I've seen worse. First we have to have lots of hot water. Mary Joe, you put some wood on the stove. I'll undress Minny May and put her to bed. You find some soft flannel cloths, Diana. I'm going to give this poor child a dose of ipecac right away."

"I've Seen Worse."

Although Minny May resisted the medicine, Anne persuaded her to take it—not only once but many times during the long anxious night. It was three o'clock in the morning when Matthew arrived with the doctor he had summoned from Spencervale. By that time Minny May was greatly improved and sleeping soundly.

"I almost gave up on Minny May, doctor," Anne confessed. "At one point it looked like she might choke to death. But when I gave her that last dose of medicine, it did the trick. You can imagine my relief. After all, there are some things that can't be expressed in words."

"Yes, I know," nodded the doctor. He was looking at Anne as if he was thinking some things that couldn't be expressed in words, either.

Later on, however, he made his sentiments known to Mr. and Mrs. Barry. "That little red-headed girl over at Green Gables is as smart as they come. I tell you she saved Minny May's

"I Almost Gave Up," Anne Confessed.

life, for it would have been too late by the time I got there."

Anne walked home on that wonderful white-faced winter morning exhausted from lack of sleep. She crawled right into bed. When she awoke, she crept downstairs and found Marilla knitting in the kitchen.

"Did you see the premier?" asked Anne at once. "What did he look like?"

"Well, he never got to be premier on account of his looks," said Marilla. "Such a nose that man had! But he can speak. I was proud of being a Conservative. Rachel Lynde, being a Liberal, had no use for him. Your lunch is in the oven, Anne, and you can help yourself to some blue plum preserves out in the pantry. Matthew told me about last night. It was certainly fortunate you knew what to do because I wouldn't have."

After Anne had eaten her lunch, Marilla said that Mrs. Barry had been over to see her. "She says you saved Minny May's life, and she

She Found Marilla Knitting in the Kitchen.

is terribly sorry for the way she acted about the currant wine. She says she knows now you didn't mean to get Diana drunk, and she hopes you'll forgive her and be good friends with Diana again. You can go visit this evening, for Diana has a bad cold and can't go out."

Oh, Marilla, can I go right now without washing my dishes? I can't think of anything so unromantic as washing dishes at this thrilling moment!"

"Yes, yes, run along," said Marilla indulgently. Then she stopped short. "Anne Shirley, come back this instant and put something on! Look at you tearing through the orchard with hair streaming. You're going to catch a death of cold."

When Anne returned to Green Gables later, she had a song in her heart. "You see before you a perfectly happy person, Marilla. Mrs. Barry had an elegant tea especially for me just as if I was real company. Nobody ever used their best china on my account before."

"Nobody Ever Used Their Best China Before."

"So you mended your fences?" Marilla asked.

"Oh, yes. Mrs. Barry kissed me and cried and said she was so sorry and that she could never repay me. I told her 'I have no hard feelings for you, Mrs. Barry. I assure you that I did not mean to intoxicate Diana, and henceforth I shall cover the past with a mantle of oblivion.' That was a pretty dignified speech, wasn't it, Marilla? And Diana and I had a wonderful afternoon together. We pledged to ask Mr. Phillips to let us sit together in school."

It wasn't long after Anne's reunion with Diana that Mr. Phillips announced he would be leaving Avonlea school in June. On his last day, all the girls were terribly upset. Even Anne came home with red eyes.

"I never knew you were so fond of Mr. Phillips," said Marilla in astonishment.

"I don't think I was crying because I was so fond of him," reflected Anne. "I just cried because all the others did. After all, Mr. Phillips

Mr. Phillips Announced He Was Leaving.

had been very mean and sarcastic to me more than once. But when he got up and made his farewell speech today and said, 'The time has come for us to part,' I felt desperately sad."

"Isn't it hard to feel desperately sad with summer vacation ahead of you?" Marilla asked.

"Oh, yes," Anne said. "Summer is such a wonderful time in Avonlea. But the highlight of the whole vacation is a special party Diana has planned the end of August at Orchard Slope. It's just for the girls in our class."

"A Wonderful Time in Avonlea"

Josie Walked the Fence.

Chapter Ten

Christmas is in the Air

Diana's party began on a high note. Everything ran smoothly until the girls went out in the garden to play a new game called "daring."

Right away, Anne dared Josie Pye to walk along the top of the board fence which enclosed the garden. To everyone's amazement Josie walked the fence as nonchalantly as if she felt the feat wasn't worth a dare. She descended from her perch flushed with victory and glared defiantly at Anne.

"So you walked a low board fence," Anne said. "I knew a girl in Marysville who could walk the ridgepole of a roof."

"I dare you to do it," Josie taunted. "I dare you to climb up and walk the ridgepole of Mr. Barry's kitchen roof."

"Don't do it, Anne," Diana begged. "You'll fall off and be killed. Never mind Josie Pye. It isn't fair to dare anybody to do anything so dangerous."

"I must do it. My honor is at stake," said Anne, turning pale. "I shall walk the ridgepole, Diana, or perish in the attempt. If I am killed, my pearl bead ring goes to you."

Anne climbed the ladder amid breathless silence, reached the ridgepole, and started to walk along it, fighting waves of dizziness. Suddenly she swayed, lost her balance, and slid down the sunbaked roof. Her friends shrieked in terror as she crashed to the ground.

If Anne had tumbled off the roof on the side where she ascended, Diana probably would have fallen heir to the pearl bead ring. Fortunately she fell on the other side where the roof

She Slid Down the Roof.

extended down over the porch so close to the ground that the fall was not a serious one.

Nevertheless, when all the girls rushed frantically around the house, they found Anne lying all white and limp in the Virginia creeper.

"Anne, are you dead?" shrieked Diana, throwing herself on her knees beside her friend. "Oh, Anne, dear Anne, say something."

To the immense relief of all the girls, especially Josie Pye, Anne sat up dizzily and answered, "No, Diana, I am not dead, but my ankle—oh, my ankle! I'm in terrible pain. Please find your father and ask him to take me home."

Marilla was in the orchard picking summer apples when she saw Mr. Barry coming over the log bridge and up the slope with Mrs. Barry beside him and a whole procession of little girls trailing after him. In his arms he carried Anne; her head lay limply against his shoulder.

"Anne, Are You Dead?"

Marilla turned white. It had been a little over a year since Anne had come to live with them. Fear stabbed suddenly at her heart. She realized that this child was dearer to her than anything else on earth.

"Mr. Barry, what has happened to Anne?" she cried, more frightened and shaken than the self-contained, sensible Marilla had been in many years.

"Don't be afraid, Marilla. I was walking the ridgepole and I fell off," Anne answered, lifting her head. "I think I may have sprained my ankle."

"I might have known you'd go and do something of the sort when I let you go to the party. Bring her in, Mr. Barry, and lay her on the sofa. Mercy me, the child has gone and fainted!"

Matthew came rushing in from the fields and raced to town to get the doctor who announced grimly after examining Anne, "I'm afraid that ankle is broken." He gave strict in-

"What Has Happened to Anne?"

structions for his patient to stay home for six to eight weeks.

At first Anne was terribly upset. This confinement meant she would miss the beginning of school and getting acquainted with the new lady teacher.

But, in the tedious weeks that followed, many friends, young and old, flocked to see her. From Mr. Bell and Josie Pye to Diana and Mrs. Allen, the new minister's wife, her visitors showered her with flowers and books and delivered news of Avonlea and school.

When at last Anne returned to school in October, she was ecstatic about her new teacher. Miss Stacy was young and sympathetic, with the ability to bring out the best in her students. Anne bloomed like a flower under her influence and carried home to the admiring Matthew and the critical Marilla glowing accounts of her school work and goals.

Of all the new projects Miss Stacy introduced, the most exciting by far was the concert

Many Friends Flocked to See Her.

to be held on Christmas night. The purpose was to raise money for the schoolhouse flag. Despite Marilla's disapproval of the event, Anne was overjoyed as she had two recitations to make.

"Oh, Marilla, I just tremble when I think of it, but it's a nice thrilly kind of tremble. Don't you hope your little Anne will distinguish herself?"

"All I hope is that you'll behave yourself. I'll be glad when all this fuss is over, and you'll be able to settle down. You are simply good for nothing just now with your head stuffed full of dialogues. It's a wonder your tongue is not clean worn out."

Anne sighed and slipped outside to where Matthew was splitting wood. Perched on a block beside him, she related every single detail regarding the Christmas recital.

"Well now, I reckon it's going to be a pretty good concert. And I expect you will say your lines just fine," Matthew said, smiling at her

She Related Every Detail.

tenderly. These two were the best of friends, but Matthew thanked his stars that he didn't have the job of raising her. That was Marilla's duty.

Yet one thing really bothered Matthew and that was the fact that Marilla dressed Anne so plainly. He first noticed just how dreary Anne's clothes were one night when she and some of her friends, all stylishly dressed, were practicing for the Christmas concert in the sitting room at Green Gables. Right then and there, he decided to give Anne a pretty dress with puffed sleeves for Christmas.

The very next day the woman-shy Matthew went to buy the dress. He deliberately chose Samuel Larson's store because he knew either Mr. Larson or his son would wait on him. To his shock, a niece of Mr. Larson's was behind the counter. Smartly dressed, she had a huge pompadour, big flirtatious brown eyes, and a dazzling smile. Matthew was so overwhelmed by her that he ordered a garden rake, hayseed,

He Went to Buy the Dress.

and finally twenty pounds of brown sugar.

"Brown sugar!" exclaimed Marilla when Matthew got home. "Whatever possessed you to get so much?"

"I guess I thought it would come in handy," said Matthew, making his escape.

Finally Matthew realized that he needed a woman to help him select a dress for Anne Since he felt Marilla would only throw cold water on the idea, he consulted Mrs. Rachel Lynde.

"Why don't I just make a dress?" Mrs. Rachel suggested. "I like sewing, and I'll make it to fit my niece, Jenny Gillis. She and Anne are as alike as two peas."

"Well now, I'm much obliged," said Matthew, "and—I dunno—but I think they make the sleeves with puffs nowadays."

"Puffs? Of course. You needn't worry a speck more about it, Matthew. I'll make it up in the very latest fashion." After he had gone, she said to herself, "Think of Matthew seeing how

Matthew Consulted Mrs. Rachel.

that poor child needed a pretty dress. Why, that man is waking up after being asleep for sixty years." On Christmas Eve, Mrs. Rachel delivered Anne's new dress to Matthew.

The next day all of Avonlea awoke to a beautiful white world. Just enough snow had fallen in the night to transform the town. Anne peered out from the frosted windows of Green Gables in delight.

"Merry Christmas, Matthew! Merry Christmas, Marilla! Isn't it a lovely white Christmas?" she cried, running downstairs. "Why, Matthew, is that for me?"

"Yes, this is my Christmas present for you," said Matthew, holding up a pale brown silk dress with two beautiful puff sleeves and rows of shirring and bows of brown silk ribbon. "Do you like it?"

"Like it! Oh, Matthew, it's perfectly exquisite," Anne said, laying the dress over a chair and clasping her hands. "Just look at those sleeves."

A Beautiful White World

"Well, well, let us eat breakfast," interrupted Marilla. "I must say, Anne, I don't think you needed that dress, but since Matthew has gotten it for you, see that you take good care of it. There's a hair ribbon Mrs. Rachel left for you. It's brown to match the dress. Come now, sit down."

"I don't see how I'm going to eat breakfast," said Anne dreamily. "Breakfast is so commonplace at such an exciting moment. I'd rather feast my eyes on that dress."

"Don't forget you have a busy day ahead of you," said Marilla. "You have to go to school and decorate the hall, and you have to have one last rehearsal before the concert tonight."

"Oh, Marilla, I'm scared," Anne cried suddenly, dropping her fork in her plate. "Suppose I forget all my lines? Suppose I open my mouth and can't speak at all?"

"Suppose I Can't Speak at All?"

Anne Was the Star.

Chapter Eleven

How Anne Got a New Hair-Do

The Christmas concert was a tremendous success. Despite Anne's stagefright, she was the star of the evening.

"Hasn't it been a wonderful night?" she sighed when it was all over, and she and Diana were walking home together under a dark, starry sky.

"I guess we must have made as much as ten dollars," Diana said. "Mr. Allan is going to send a write-up about it to the Charlottetown paper."

"Oh, Diana, will we really see our names in

print? Your solo was perfectly elegant. I was so proud of you!"

"And your recitations simply brought down the house, Anne."

"Oh, I was so nervous. I felt as if a million eyes were looking at me, and for one dreadful moment, I was sure I couldn't begin at all. Then I thought of my new puff sleeves and took courage. I knew I had to live up to those sleeves."

That night after Anne had gone to bed, Matthew and Marilla sat talking by the kitchen fire.

"Well now, I guess Anne did as well as any of them," said Matthew.

"Yes, she did," admitted Marilla. "She is a bright child. And she looked real nice, too. I was kind of opposed to this concert scheme, but I guess there's no harm in it. Anyhow, I was proud of Anne tonight, although I'm not going to tell her so."

"I did tell her so," Matthew said, "right be-

Talking by the Fire

fore she went to bed."

"She'll be thirteen in March," Marilla commented. "I suppose we should be thinking about sending her to Queen's Academy. But there's plenty of time to decide about that."

The winter weeks slipped quietly by. January turned into February, and February turned into March. Early in the month Anne celebrated her birthday with Diana.

"Just think, I'm thirteen years old today," Anne said to her best friend. "I can scarcely believe I'm in my teens. When I awoke this morning, it seemed that everything must be different. In two more years I'll be really grown-up."

In many respects Anne was already quite mature. She was a highly disciplined student who enjoyed writing compositions so much that she founded a story club. The group, composed of Diana, Ruby Gillis, Jane Andrews and Anne, met in the afternoons after school to write fiction on a regular basis.

"I'm 13 Years Old Today."

"It's extremely interesting," Anne told Marilla. "Each girl has to read her story out loud, and then we all discuss it. They all do pretty well, but I have to tell them what to write about. That isn't hard because I have millions of ideas."

"Such foolishness," scoffed Marilla. "You're wasting time you should be spending on your lessons."

"But we're careful to put a moral in each story," explained Anne. "All the good people are rewarded and all the bad ones are punished. I do try to be a good person myself, but it's so hard. I hope to be like Mrs. Allan when I grow up. Do you think there is a chance of that, Marilla?"

"I shouldn't say there was a great deal," Marilla snapped. "I'm sure Mrs. Allan was never such a silly, forgetful girl as you are."

"No, but she wasn't always as good as she is now either," Anne said seriously. "She told me herself that she was very mischievous when

"Such Foolishness."

she was a girl and was always getting into scrapes."

Like every teen-age girl growing up, Anne continued to get into her share of scrapes, too. Late one afternoon in April, Marilla returned home from a meeting of the Ladies' Aid Society expecting to find Anne at work in the kitchen and the table all set for dinner. To her dismay, the fire was out and Anne was nowhere in sight.

"That girl is gadding about somewhere with Diana, writing stories or some other tomfoolery and forgetting all about her duties," Marilla complained to Matthew who had just come in from plowing. "I must say I've never known Anne to be untrustworthy before."

"Well now, I dunno," said Matthew. "Don't call her untrustworthy until you're sure she's disobeyed you. Mebbe it can all be explained."

Marilla prepared supper, washed and dried the dishes all in grim silence. Still there was no sign of Anne.

"That Girl Is Gadding About Somewhere."

In search of a candle to light the cellar, Marilla went up to Anne's room. When she lit the candle on the bedside table, she saw Anne lying facedown in the pillows.

"Mercy on us," cried the astonished Marilla. "Have you been asleep, Anne?"

"No, and I'm not sick either. Please go away, Marilla, and don't look at me."

"Anne Shirley, what is the matter with you? Get up this minute and tell me."

"Look at my hair," Anne whispered.

"Why, it's green!" cried Marilla, looking at Anne's hair, flowing in heavy masses down her back.

"Yes, it's green," moaned the distraught girl. "I thought nothing could be as bad as red hair. But this is ten times worse. I'm sorry now that I dyed it."

"Dyed it! Dyed your hair? Well," said Marilla sarcastically, "if I were going to dye my hair, I wouldn't have dyed it green."

"But I didn't mean to dye it green," Anne ex-

"Don't Look at Me."

plained. "I bought this dye from a peddler who promised me my hair would be a raven black. He swore the color would not wash out."

Time proved that the peddler was right on one point. The color was permanent. Despite the fact Anne hid away at home for a week and washed and scrubbed her hair every day, the color remained a ghastly yellow-green.

"It's no use, Anne. That is fast dye if there ever was any," Marilla said one afternoon. "Your hair must be cut off; there is no other way."

"All right. Just do it and get it over with, Marilla," Anne pleaded.

Picking up her scissors, Marilla shingled Anne's hair as closely to her head as possible. The mortified teen-ager looked in the mirror once, screamed and swore she'd never look again.

Anne's clipped head created a sensation at school when she returned. To her relief no one guessed she had dyed her hair green—not

Picking Up Her Scissors

even Josie Pye who told her she looked like a perfect scarecrow.

"Diana says that when my hair begins to grow, I should wear a black velvet ribbon around my head with a bow on the side," Anne told Marilla, who was lying on the sofa late one afternoon nursing one of her headaches. "She thinks it will be very becoming."

Fortunately Anne's hair grew rapidly. As it grew in, it formed soft, silky curls all over her head. As Diana had suggested, Anne wore a black velvet ribbon to keep it in place.

"Your hair is real pretty now. I'd say it has turned a true auburn," Diana said to Anne one day when the story club met at the pond at Orchard Slope to act out Tennyson's poem "Elaine", which they had learned in school. "You get my vote to play the beautiful lily maid, Elaine."

Ruby Gillis and Jane Andrews both agreed. Thrilled to be cast as the lead character, Anne threw a faded piano shawl around her neck

Anne's Hair Grew Rapidly.

and leaped into an old rowboat. Immediately her companions pushed the craft into the current in the direction of the bridge. Then, they went flying through the woods to meet her on the other side of the bridge.

To her horror, Anne looked down and saw that water was rushing into the boat through a hole in the bottom. She remembered the oars had been left behind on the landing. Luckily, the boat floated close to the bridge. She jumped out onto a tree trunk pile and held on as tightly as she could.

As Anne watched the rowboat sink beneath the murky water, she called out to her friends. But no one heard her, and no one came to her rescue.

Water Was Rushing In.

They Charged Through the Woods.

Chapter Twelve

The Dream of a Lifetime

Diana, Ruby and Jane had seen the rowboat sink and assumed that Anne was in it. Screaming in terror, they charged through the woods to get help—never once glancing in the direction of the bridge.

Anne's imagination ran wild. Suppose nobody ever came! Suppose she grew so tired and cramped that she could hold on no longer! She looked down into the wicked green depths below her, wavering with oily shadows, and shivered.

Then, just as she thought she could not endure the pain in her arms and wrists one more moment, a little dory appeared from under the bridge. At the the helm was none other than Gilbert Blythe!

"Anne Shirley! How on earth did you get there?" he exclaimed, looking up into her big, frightened but scornful eyes.

Without waiting for an answer, he pulled close to the pile and extended his hand. Clinging to him, Anne scrambled down into the dory where she sat embarrassed and furious in her dripping wet shawl.

"What happened, Anne?" asked Gilbert, taking up the oars.

"We were playing 'Elaine'", explained Anne, "and I had to drift down to Camelot in the barge—I mean, the rowboat. It began to leak, and I climbed out on the pile. I don't know where my friends went. Now will you be kind enough to row me to the landing?"

Gilbert rowed to the landing and got out to help Anne off. "Look here," he said suddenly,

Anne Scrambled into the Dory.

"Can't we be friends? I'm awfully sorry I made fun of your hair in school that time. It was such a long time ago. Besides I think your hair is very pretty now. What do you say?"

At first Anne's heart gave a quick little beat. But then she remembered vividly how Gilbert had humiliated her before the whole school. "No," she said coldly. "I will never be friends with you—not ever."

"All right!" Gilbert said, springing into his boat angrily. "You can be sure I'll never ask you again."

Gilbert had barely rowed away than Diana and Jane came rushing up, relieved to see their lily maid alive and in one piece.

"Oh, Anne, there was no one home at Orchard Slope or Green Gables to help us," Diana cried. "Thank heaven you're all right!"

"How did you escape?" Jane wanted to know.

"I climbed up on one of the piles," explained Anne wearily. "Gilbert Blythe came along in a dory and brought me to shore."

"I Will Never Be Friends—Not Ever."

"Oh, Anne, how romantic," cried Jane. "Of course you'll speak to him after this."

"No, I won't," retorted Anne, "and I don't want to hear the word romantic again, Jane Andrews. This experience has cured me forever of being a romantic."

Marilla was terribly annoyed with Anne over this latest escapade and scolded her soundly. The truth was she had grown to love this slim, gray-eyed girl more than life itself. The strength of her love frightened her, and as a result she hid her feelings.

Unfortunately, Anne had no idea how much Marilla adored her. For the most part she viewed her new mother as someone hard to please and totally lacking in sympathy and understanding.

Therefore, Anne was very surprised when Marilla talked to her one day that fall about studying for the entrance exam to Queen's Teaching Academy.

"Miss Stacy came over to talk to Matthew

"How Romantic!"

and me about it today," Marilla explained. "She wants to organize a class of her advanced students and give them extra lessons after school. Would you like to go to Queen's, Anne?"

"Oh, Marilla," Anne cried, "it's the dream of my lifetime to be a teacher. But isn't it terribly expensive?"

"You needn't worry about that part of it. Matthew and I want you to have a good education and be in a position to support yourself. You'll always have a home at Green Gables as long as we are alive, but this is an uncertain world. So you can join the Queen's class if you like. You will have a year and a half to prepare for the entrance exams."

And so it was that the Queen's class was organized. Gilbert Blythe, Anne Shirley, Ruby Gillis, Jane Andrews, Josie Pye, Charlie Sloane, and Moody Spurgeon MacPherson all joined. Diana Barry did not, a situation which made Anne very sad.

From the beginning Anne and Gilbert were

"The Dream of My Lifetime."

the leaders of the class. The tremendous rivalry between them increased, but beyond that Gilbert completely ignored Anne. Suddenly she discovered that it wasn't pleasant to be ignored. She also realized that somewhere along the line she *had* forgiven Gilbert. "Too bad it was too late," she thought.

Otherwise the school year passed along in a round of pleasant duties and studies. Anne was happy, eager and interested. There were lessons to be learned and honors to be won, delightful books to read, new pieces to be practiced for the Sunday School choir, and pleasant Saturday afternoons to be spent with Mrs. Allan at the manse.

In the spring a rumor circulated that Miss Stacy had been offered a teaching position in her own home district. When the Queen's class asked her about it, she told them that she was much too interested in them to even think of leaving Avonlea.

"I'm so glad," said Anne with shining eyes.

With Mrs. Allan at the Manse

"Dear Miss Stacy, it would be perfectly dreadful if you didn't come back. I don't believe I would have the heart to go on with my studies if another teacher came here."

When school opened in the fall the Queen's class knew they had to study hard in order to pass the entrance examinations which were not far off now. Anne had bad dreams where she found herself staring miserably at pass lists where Gilbert's name was blazoned at the top and hers did not appear at all.

Despite the pressure the entrance exams posed, the school year was interesting and the days just seemed to fly by. This was due largely to Miss Stacy's careful guidance. She led her class to think and explore and discover for themselves to a degree that quite shocked Mrs. Rachel Lynde and the school trustees who were highly suspicious of any new methods of teaching.

That winter Anne shot up in height so rapidly that Marilla was astonished one day, when

The Days Flew By.

they were standing side by side, to find the girl was taller than herself.

"Why Anne, how you've grown," she said. The child she had learned to love had vanished and in her place was a tall, serious young girl of fifteen. Marilla knew she would miss her terribly if she went away to school next year.

As the time to take the exams drew near, Marilla could see that Anne was worried. "How do you think you'll do?" she asked her.

"Sometimes I think I'll do all right—and then I get horribly afraid. We've studied hard and Miss Stacy has drilled us thoroughly. Oh, it would be a disgrace if I fail, especially if Gil—I mean if the others passed."

But Anne also wanted to do well for the sake of Marilla and Matthew who had done so much for her. In June the class spent a long, hard week in Charlottetown taking the entrance exams at the Academy. Competition was keen as there were students from all over Prince Edward Island.

"How You've Grown."

When it was all over, Anne thought she did well in everything but geometry. Her main hope was that she would pass and come out ahead of Gilbert. Unfortunately the pass list was not to be announced for two weeks. "How am I *ever* going to stand the suspense?" she wondered.

Anne Thought She Did Well.

Shaking Hands and Sinking Feelings

Chapter Thirteen

An Ending and a Beginning

After two weeks Anne, Jane, Ruby, and Josie began haunting the post office and opening the Charlottetown paper with shaking hands and cold, sinking feelings as bad as any they had experienced during entrance week.

When three weeks had slipped by without the pass list appearing, Anne began to feel she couldn't stand the strain much longer. Her appetite failed, and she lost all interest in Avonlea doings. Noting how dejected she was every afternoon when she dragged home from the post office, Matthew couldn't help but worry about her.

Then one evening the news came. Anne was sitting at the open window of her bedroom, drinking in the beauty of the summer dusk. Suddenly she spotted Diana flying down through the firs, over the log bridge, and up the slope, with a fluttering newspaper in her hand.

"Anne, you passed!" cried Diana, dashing into her room a few minutes later. "You and Gilbert tied for first place, but your name is first on the list—first on a list of two hundred. Everyone else in the class here passed, too. Father just brought home the paper not ten minutes ago."

"I never dreamed of this," said Anne, picking up the newspaper. "Yes, I did too, just once. But it seemed so vain and presumptuous to think I could lead Prince Edward Island. Oh, Di, I must go tell Matthew."

The two girls hurried to the field below the barn where Matthew was raking hay. As luck

"Anne, You Passed!" Cried Diana.

would have it, Mrs. Rachel and Marilla were chatting at the lane fence.

"Matthew," cried Anne. "I passed. I came in first!"

"Well now, I always said it," said Matthew, gazing at the pass list in delight.

"You've done pretty well, I must say, Anne," beamed Marilla, trying to hide her pride in Anne from her critical friend.

"I guess she has done well, and far be it for me not to say so," said Mrs. Rachel generously. "You're a credit to your friends, young lady, and we're all proud of you."

After the news of Anne's acceptance to Queen's, the Cuthberts put all their energy into getting her ready to leave that fall. Anne's wardrobe for college was not only ample, but all the new clothes were stylish and pretty. Matthew saw to that.

"This green dress is perfectly lovely," said Anne one night as she modeled a frilly silk party dress for Matthew and Marilla in the

"I Came in First!"

kitchen. The gown was a special gift from Marilla, who had it custom made for evening events.

"It's the perfect thing to wear if you're asked to recite poetry at any concerts at Queen's," Marilla said. "I'm sure you will be because you have made quite a name for yourself around the Island. Who could ever forget the night you recited "The Maiden's Vow" to that packed audience in Charlottetown? My, there seems to be no end to our being proud of you!"

"Why, Marilla, I think you're crying," said Anne, kissing her tenderly. "Are you upset because I'm going away? I shall always be your own little Anne who will love you and Matthew more and better every day of her life!"

Fighting the tears himself, Matthew got up quickly and hurried outside where he sat under a poplar tree and remembered the sad, frightened orphan girl he had brought to Green Gables four years before and how she had changed their lives.

"Are You Upset Because I'm Going Away?"

"Well now, I guess my putting my oar in occasionally never did any harm," he thought. "She's smart and pretty and loving, too. She's been a blessing to us, and there never was a luckier mistake than the one Mrs. Spencer made. It was Providence that brought Anne to us. The Almighty saw how much we needed her."

The September day finally arrived when Anne said good-bye to a tearful Diana and a solemn Marilla and set off with Matthew to officially enter Queen's in Charlottetown.

The first day at the Academy passed pleasantly enough in a whirl of excitement. Anne was busy meeting all the new students, learning to recognize professors, and signing up for classes.

Both Anne and Gilbert registered for Second Year work as Miss Stacy had suggested. This meant getting a First Class teacher's license in one year instead of two. It also meant a harder work load. Jane, Ruby, Josie, Charlie,

There Never Was a Luckier Mistake.

and Moody all signed up to take the Second Class work.

Consequently, Anne found herself to be a stranger in a class of fifty students. The only person she knew was her old rival, Gilbert. "My, he looks determined," she thought. "I suppose he's already made up his mind to win the medal."

Homesickness struck Anne at night when she was alone in her room at the boarding house. Although Josie Pye had never been a favorite of hers, Anne was glad to see her when she dropped by unexpectedly.

"You've been crying," remarked Josie, staring at Anne's red eyes. "I guess you're homesick. So many people have so little self-control in that respect. I have no intention of being homesick. This town is much more fun than that pokey old Avonlea. Oh, did you hear that Queen's is going to offer one of the Avery scholarships? The Board of Governors will announce it tomorrow."

The Only Person She Knew Was Gilbert.

Before Josie told her the news, Anne had been aspiring for a teacher's license, First Class, at the end of the year and perhaps the medal. But now in one moment she had a new dream—winning the Avery scholarship, enabling her to take a four year arts course at Redmond College, and receiving her B. A. degree.

The scholarship, which paid two hundred fifty dollars a year for four years, would be awarded to the June graduate with the highest marks in English and English literature. While these were Anne's best subjects, she knew she would have to work harder than ever before to win.

Anne's homesickness wore off largely because of weekend visits home. As long as the good weather lasted, the Avonlea students took the train home every Friday night. Diana and other old friends were always there to greet them, catch up on their news, and walk them to their houses.

She Had a New Dream.

However, after the Christmas holidays the Avonlea crowd stayed on campus on weekends and buckled down to work. Certain facts had been generally accepted. The medal contestants had been narrowed down to three—Gilbert, Anne, and Lewis Wilson. Of the six students who were considered to be in the running for the Avery scholarship, a girl named Emily Clay was thought to be the top candidate.

Night after night during the long winter, Anne stayed up into the wee hours pouring over her lessons and laboring over her compositions. Still she didn't have high hopes of winning the scholarship because Emily Clay always spoke up so brilliantly in class and continued to get high marks.

Then almost before anybody knew it, spring had come to Charlottetown. Unfortunately all the harassed students thought or talked about were their upcoming exams. For Anne, exam week was a grueling ordeal. She was glad

Night After Night of the Long Winter

when it was over.

On the morning when the final results of the exams were posted, Anne and Jane walked together to the administration building at Queen's.

"I have no hope of winning the Avery," Anne said as they walked in the door, "but the medal is certainly a possibility. Oh, I don't have the courage to go look at the bulletin board in front of everyone and see who won. Promise me you will go do it for me."

It turned out that that wasn't necessary. The hall was full of boys who were carrying Gilbert on their shoulders and yelling at the top of their lungs, "Hurrah for Blythe, medalist!"

Pale and shaken, Anne felt the sickening pangs of defeat and heartbreak. She had failed; Gilbert had won. And Matthew had been so sure she would win the medal.

The Hall Was Full of Boys.

"Winner of the Avery!"

Chapter Fourteen

The Bend in the Road

As Anne and Jane started to walk out of the building, somebody suddenly cried, "Three cheers for Anne Shirley, winner of the Avery!"

Excited friends surrounded the two girls, congratulating Anne enthusiastically. Her shoulders were squeezed and her hands shaken over and over. Throughout it all, she managed to whisper to Jane, "Won't Matthew and Marilla be pleased? I must write to them right away!" Tears of joy filled her eyes.

Commencement, the next important happening, was held in the assembly hall at the

Academy. Addresses were given, essays read, songs sung, and the public award of diplomas, prizes and medals made.

Matthew and Marilla were there, with eyes for only one student on the platform, a tall girl in pale green, who read the best essay and was named the winner of the prized Avery scholarship.

"Reckon you're glad we kept her, Marilla?" whispered Matthew, nudging his sister.

"Stuff and nonsense. It's not the first time I've been glad," Marilla snapped back.

Anne went home to Avonlea with her family that evening. She had not been at Green Gables since April and was thrilled to see Diana again.

The next morning at breakfast it suddenly struck Anne that Matthew was not looking well. Marilla confirmed Anne's suspicions and admitted that Matthew had had some bad spells with his heart that spring.

She also confessed that her headaches were

A Tall Girl in Pale Green

occurring more frequently and that her new glasses had not done any good. However, she promised Anne she would consult a well-known oculist who was coming to the Island soon.

In early evening Anne went with Matthew to bring in the cows. He walked slowly back through the woods with his head bent. Anne walked in step with him, drinking in the beautiful sunset.

"You've been working too hard lately, Matthew," she chided him. "Why don't you take life easier?"

"Well now, I can't seem to," said Matthew, as he opened the gate to let the cows through. "Guess I'm just used to working hard."

"If I had been the boy you sent for," said Anne wistfully, "I'd be able to help you now."

"I'd rather have you than a dozen boys, Anne," said Matthew, patting her hand. "After all, it wasn't a boy who won the Avery scholarship. It was my girl—my girl who I'm so

Drinking in the Beautiful Sunset

proud of."

He smiled his shy smile at her and went in the yard. Anne took the memory of that moment with her when she went to her room that night. She sat for a long time thinking of the past and dreaming of the future.

The next morning as she came through the front hall, her hands full of narcissi, she heard Marilla cry out, "Matthew—Matthew—what's the matter? Are you sick?"

Matthew, his face drawn and gray, staggered back and forth in the porch doorway, a folded newspaper in his hand. Anne and Marilla rushed to his side, but before they could reach him, he collapsed.

"He's fainted," gasped Marilla. "Anne, run for Martin. Quick! He's at the barn."

Martin, the hired man, started at once for the doctor, calling at Orchard Slope on his way to send Mr. and Mrs. Barry over. Mrs. Rachel, who was there visiting, came too. They found Anne and Marilla desperately trying to revive

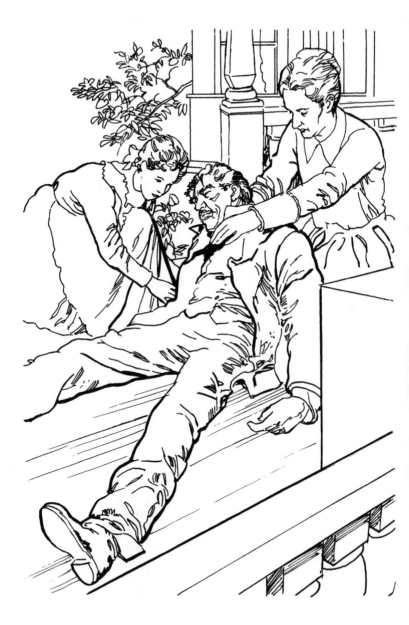

He Collapsed.

Matthew.

"Oh, Marilla," Mrs. Rachel said gravely, taking Matthew's pulse. "I don't think we can do anything for him."

When the doctor came, he said that death had been instant and was probably caused by a sudden shock. The shock turned out to be the failure of the bank which Matthew had just read about in the paper. Every penny of Cuthbert money was gone.

The news of Matthew's death spread quickly through Avonlea. All day friends and neighbors thronged Green Gables on errands of kindness. When night fell, the house was hushed and silent. The Barrys and Mrs. Rachel stayed until Marilla and Anne at last went to bed.

In the middle of the night, Anne awoke. She remembered Matthew's words, "My girl—my girl who I'm proud of." Then the tears came uncontrollably, as she gave in to her grief.

The days and weeks passed slowly after the

Every Penny Was Gone.

funeral. Anne planted a white rosebush at Matthew's grave and went there often to tend the plot.

One afternoon when she returned home, she found Marilla sitting very dejectedly in the kitchen. "Are you tired?" Anne asked.

"It's not that. I saw the eye doctor today. He says that if I give up nearly all my activities and wear new glasses, my eyes may not get worse. Otherwise I'll be stone blind in six months."

"Marilla, you mustn't think the worst," Anne said, stunned. "The doctor has given you hope."

I don't call it much hope," said Marilla bitterly. "What is there to live for if I can't use my eyes? I think I'm going to have to sell the farm and board somewhere—maybe with Rachel. Thank heaven you have that scholarship."

"You can't sell Green Gables," Anne cried, her mind whirling. "I won't let you lose your home!"

A White Rosebush

"I wish I didn't have to," Marilla lamented, "but you can see I can't live here alone. And eventually my eyesight will go."

"You won't have to stay here by yourself. I'll live with you. I'm not going to Redmond," Anne declared.

"Not going to Redmond? What do you mean?"

"Just what I say. Marilla, surely you don't think I would leave you alone in your trouble after all you've done for me? I'm sure Mr. Barry will rent the farm, and I can teach either in Avonlea or Carmody. I'll keep you cheered up and we'll be cozy and happy together."

"Oh, Anne, it sounds wonderful. But I can't let you sacrifice your dream of college for me."

"It's no sacrifice. I can study college courses right here at home. The worst thing we could possibly do is to give up Green Gables. I'm sixteen and a half now, and my mind is made up."

"You blessed girl!" said Marilla, throwing

"Not Going to Redmond?"

her arms around Anne, "you have given me new life. I love you for it, but then I've always loved you. I just was never able to say it before." Anne quickly returned the hug, and they both cried a little.

When it became known around Avonlea that Anne Shirley had given up the idea of going to college and intended to stay home and teach, there was a lot of talk about it. Most of the good folks, not knowing about Marilla's eyes, thought Anne was foolish. However, Mrs. Allan told her she had done a wonderful thing.

Mrs. Rachel also had plenty to say. "Well, Anne, I was glad to hear you have given up your notion of going to college. You've got as much education as a woman can be comfortable with."

In the next breath she informed Anne that the trustees had given her the post at Avonlea school. Apparently Gilbert had submitted his application but withdrawn it when he heard about Anne's situation. He planned to teach at

The Trustees Had Given Her the Post.

White Sands.

Deeply touched by Gilbert's sacrifice, Anne stopped by the Blythe home to thank him. "It was very good of you to give up so much for me. I really appreciate it."

"I was glad I was able to do you some small service, Anne. I hope this means we can forget the past and be good friends."

"Gil, I've been a silly goose. I hope you can forgive me."

"We are going to be the best of friends," said Gil jubilantly. "We were born to be good friends, Anne. You've thwarted destiny long enough. I know we can help each other in many ways. You are going to keep up your studies, aren't you? So am I. Come, I'm going to walk home with you."

Gilbert and Anne walked slowly back to Green Gables, pausing at the gate and talking on and on as if to make up for lost time.

When he left, Anne stood at the gate thinking. "When I left Queen's, my future stretched

"I've Been a Silly Goose."

before me like a straight road. Now there's a bend in it. I don't know what lies around the bend, but I believe in my dreams and ideals. Nothing can take those from me. God's in his heaven; all's right in the world."

She went slowly inside.

"I Believe in My Dreams."